Me, Too!
Creative Crafts
for Preschoolers

ANYTIME ★ CRAFTS

Dedication

To my granddaughters, Amy and Bethany Whiteside,
and their friend, Katie Warner, who made the crafts
to test my directions

To Lucile Fallon, who did the proofreading

To Jo Warner, who critiqued and encouraged

And to my husband Lorin, who cooked the meals
so I could stay at the computer.

Me, Too!

Creative Crafts for Preschoolers

Crafts for ages 3 to 5

Sarah H. Healton, Ed. D.
Kay Healton Whiteside
Illustrations by Grace Meyer

TAB BOOKS
Blue Ridge Summit, PA

FIRST EDITION
SECOND PRINTING

© 1992 by **TAB Books**.
TAB Books is a division of McGraw-Hill, Inc.

Library of Congress Cataloging-in-Publication Data

Healton, Sarah H.
    Me, too! : creative crafts for preschoolers / by Sarah H. Healton.
        p.   cm.
    Includes index.
    ISBN 0-8306-4041-X   ISBN 0-8306-4042-8 (pbk.)
    1. Handicraft.   2. Creative activities and seat work.   I. Title.
TT157.H369   1992
745.5—dc20   92-7289
                                                    CIP

Acquisitions Editor: Stacy Varavvas-Pomeroy
Editor: April D. Nolan
Director of Production: Katherine G. Brown
Page Makeup: Janice Ridenour
Book Design: Jaclyn J. Boone
Cover Design: Denny Bond, East Petersburg, Pa.
Cover Photo: Susan Riley, Harrisonburg, Va.   TAB1

Contents

MAKING THINGS FOR
SPECIAL DAYS

Introduction

Facing a room of preschoolers about to be armed with scissors and glue is not as scary as it sounds. Take heart! Everyone can go home with a completed craft, a sense of accomplishment, and a smile on his or her face—even you.

That's because *Me, Too! Creative Crafts for Preschoolers* is far more than just another craft book. This book helps you select the craft best suited to your children's age group by giving you an idea of what you can expect a child to be able to do at each age level.

We know that young children learn by imitating the people around them. They often say, "Me, too!" when they see someone doing something they want to do. We also know that some children mature faster than others, and that boys tend to develop their large muscles ahead of girls. Nonetheless, the joy of creating exists in all children. The crafts in this book encourage children to:

- use attention skills
- develop their eye and hand coordination
- practice left and right
- develop two-handed coordination
- obey safety rules
- develop scissors skills
- match shapes, sizes, and colors
- develop memory skills

Children need lots of fun experiences developing these skills. Those who have not had enough experience practicing these basic skills will frequently have trouble learning to read.

Making crafts also develops each child's need for self-expression and manipulation. For example, making a face on a paper plate looks easy—and it is. With good directions and a little supervision, even 3-year-olds can do it. When they are finished, though, they have far more than just a craft; they also have learned:

- how parts of the face go together
- the correct names of body parts
- how to arrange and glue objects on a paper plate
- the difference between left and right
- how to combine different shapes to look like a face

Every craft in this book can be made easily by children ages 3 to 5, with adult supervision. Each project lists the basic tools and materials you will need (per child), and some offer variations of the project so you can expand on the same idea.

Not only will this book provide you with lots of fun activities to share with your preschoolers, but it will also provide your children with a sense of accomplishment. So what are you waiting for? Read the *How to Use this Book* section, and start making crafts together!

How to use this book

This book is more than just another craft book. It not only helps you select a craft best suited for your age group, but it also gives you an idea of what you can expect a child to be able to do at each age. With adult supervision, all the projects in this book can be made easily by 3- to 5-year-olds. In addition, the children will learn, expand, or practice a number of skills through making these crafts. Most importantly, the children will develop a positive self image when they complete a project and have something tangible to show for it.

Age group & icons

For your particular age group, see the chart on page xvi in the *To the adult* section regarding what skills children have at certain ages and which projects develop these skills. In addition, the crafts are rated by age under the heading of each project.

Each craft in this book is rated by icons for:

Prior adult preparation required

Inexpensive materials

Less than 30 minutes to complete

Ease with a large group

Non-messy

Materials & tools lists

A list of the necessary tools and materials required for each craft *per child* is included at the beginning of each project. Generally speaking, the *materials* required will include those things that are used up during the making of the project. The *tools*, on the other hand, will be those things that will still be intact when the craft has been completed, such as scissors, bottles of glue, and felt-tip markers.

The "I learned" section

This section is easy to find and is included with every project. Even non-reading children can recognize the phrase "I learned . . ." when it is repeated, and that repetition will help them understand some of the basic principles of language (such as noun/verb combinations in sentences). Read this section to the children once they have made the craft, and encourage them to add other things they learned. After you have read it once, ask the children to read it back to you; this will increase their eye span and prepare them (subtly) for reading.

Children with special needs

Most preschool children have the skills needed to make the crafts in this book, and they will get lots of practice refining these skills while making these crafts. Other children, however, might have greater difficulty mastering the more complicated crafts skills, and they might need more patience and guidance from you as the adult.

- awkward children
- shy children
- children who confuse right and left
- children who reverse letters and numbers
- children with short attention spans
- aggressive children

The awkward child

The awkward child has trouble skipping, running, hopping, throwing, and catching. This child also has trouble cutting, holding a pencil, and coloring between the lines. This child has difficulty recognizing body parts and needs to experience how body parts connect. The crafts in the *Learning About Me* section are designed to help with these concepts and will help a child understand: body image and body sizes, left and right concepts, relative positions (such as under, over, above, below, behind, and between), and how body parts fit together.

The awkward child needs lots of practice tracing and cutting out large objects such as circles and squares. The craft *Stuffed Fish & Other Animals* gives the awkward child many opportunities to practice using large muscles by finger painting, tracing, and cutting, as well as stuffing.

The shy child

The shy child needs lots of personal attention and frequent praise for tasks accomplished. Because shy children are quiet and demand little attention, they are easy to overlook, so be on the lookout for them.

Playing with puppets, such as the ones in the *Puppets I Can Make* section, encourages a shy child to use imagination. With a puppet, a shy child can become anybody he or she wishes. Using puppets also helps to develop language by encouraging a child to talk to other children, or even to talk over a problem with a teacher or parent.

The child who confuses left and right

By age 5 children will prefer to use one hand over the other. Most children prefer the right hand, but left-handed children should stay left-handed. Don't make any attempt to change them; naturally left-handed children forced to use their right hands frequently develop a stutter.

No clear preference for the right or left hand by age 5 is called *mixed dominance*, and it can lead to confusion when learning to read. These children might see letters backwards and reverse their order—such as *saw* and *was*. Stringing beans in a pattern, making paper chains, and following directions that involve left and right are good activities for these children. (See the skills chart in the *To the Adult* section for specific projects.) If a child picks up a pencil most of the time with the right hand, he or she should practice that preference until the dominance is firmly established.

The child who reverses letters & numbers

The child who reverses letters or numbers needs practice playing sequence games and following easy oral directions. These children might have trouble distinguishing the letters b and d or p and q, or turning letters s and r the right direction.

Such children need to see, hear, and feel the shapes of different letters. They also need to practice games and activities where left and right are emphasized (such as shaking hands or dancing the hokey-pokey).

Roll long snakes out of clay or play dough, to make letters such as b or d. The child can feel the shape of the letters. Have the child trace the shape with a finger until he or she can draw it correctly in the air with closed eyes.

The child with a short attention span

Children with short attention spans need lots of personal attention and frequent praise for completing each part of a task. You can make an attempt to shorten craft projects for such children—for example, have them make necklaces with only three beads instead of with ten or more. A catch-and-toss game also provides excellent practice for increasing the short attention span.

The aggressive child

The aggressive child is easy to spot. Almost every group has one or more of these. This child wants to be first, shows-off, demands attention, frequently grabs supplies away from other children, talks too loud, throws things, or uses supplies in an inappropriate manner.

For these children, decide on a definite plan of action beforehand, especially if more than one adult is working with the group. These children have learned how to get their own way by pitting one adult against the other, so they need to know what is expected and what is not acceptable. For example, if you define the rule that no child is allowed to poke another child with scissors or other sharp objects, you will have established at least one specific boundary for the children.

Be sure all the children in the group understand what materials they can use and which ones only the leaders will use. The children will have greater security when they know what they can and cannot do.

Praise the children who work quietly or wait their turns. Withhold supplies from a demanding child until the others have received theirs.

If an aggressive child acts in a way that could hurt himself or another child, remove the aggressive child from the group immediately. Place a chair away from the group where this child can sit until he or she is ready to come back into the group and participate in an appropriate manner.

When this child is ready to return (and you are ready to have the child return) to the group, give the child the supplies needed to make the craft. Praise the child for each part of the craft completed, but give the child attention and praise only when he or she behaves in an acceptable manner. If the rest of the group has moved to another step of the craft, do not stop the group's progress to catch up the aggressive child. Inappropriate behavior was his choice—going home with an incomplete craft is also his choice.

As the child leaves, remind him or her that at the next meeting, you hope he or she will be ready to listen and to follow directions so he or she will have a completed craft to take home.

To the adult

Good planning, having the necessary supplies on hand, and a good sense of humor should make for a happy craft experience for both you and the children. In addition, the knowledge of the appropriate craft for the particular age level of the children should keep everyone from being frustrated. This section will give you an idea of what skills develop when, and what crafts might be appropriate for your group of children. Select a craft that will not only be fun, but will also help the children learn.

Of course, some children are ahead of others in their coordination and maturity. Nonetheless, it will help you to know the average age certain skills develop. For more information about what skills are practiced in the particular crafts in this book, see the skills chart at the end of this section.

A cautionary word

Children at this young age are still orally fixated: They will put anything they can reach into their mouths. To prevent choking, make sure that beads, buttons, and other such objects are at least 1 inch across. Materials such as clay and paint should be from supplies clearly labeled nontoxic. The recipe for play dough in this book is edible; however, it contains such a large amount of salt that no child will want to eat very much.

Age three

In the third year of life, large muscle development continues. A 3-year-old should be able to pedal a tricycle and to throw and bounce a ball (although catching will still be difficult). A 3-year-old needs to be encouraged to:
- pound and mold clay
- experiment with color by painting with large brushes
- fill bean bags with beans to use for throwing and catching

Fine muscle development begins at age 3, and children should practice grasping large crayons to scribble, using blunt scissors to cut shapes, and copying a circle.

Body concept also begins, as children become aware that arms are attached to their bodies, not their heads, and so on. Most 3-year-olds can also name the parts of the body, such as nose, knees, fingers, etc., but might misplace them in a drawing.

A 3-year-old child should understand the difference between big and little and high and low, and he should be aware of how things feel (soft, hard, wet, rough).

Children at age 3 are also developing a sense of sequence. Crafts provide an opportunity for the child to:

- count (most can count to three; some can count to five)
- follow the sequence for making the craft
- place craft materials in an order or pattern

Three-year-olds also need to fine-tune the skill of following simple directions. As they make the crafts in this book, they will practice listening to directions, finding and picking up the objects needed to start, and completing each step in the right order.

Finally, at age 3, a child's vocabulary is expanding greatly, and he or she will speak with simple sentences.

Age four

At age 4, big muscle development continues. Four-year-olds can throw and catch a ball or other objects, so bean bags are an excellent craft to make for throwing and catching. Children at age 4 can also climb quickly, hang from bars on a jungle gym, build things or objects with blocks, and walk a balance beam. They enjoy playing circle games, dancing, painting, drawing, and matching objects.

Because small muscle development has begun, 4-year-olds should be able to:

- use crayons and pencils to draw a circle or a line
- trace outline of an object, such as drawing a line around an animal shape
- use scissors
- cut and paste
- use hammer on a pounding board
- begin to lace shoes, tie knots, button clothes, zip zippers
- build with pegs and tinker toys
- make animals with clay or play dough

Body concept increases at the age of 4. Children at this age should know how to move parts of the body together (to make angels in the snow, for example). They should also be able to learn simple dance steps and respond to music.

Four-year-olds should be able to count to 10; a good way to practice this is to have them count the objects they will need for each craft. You can also have them name objects in sequence (such as, "one large bead, two small ones"), match patterns, or string beads (or macaroni) in a pattern.

Children in this age group can not only follow verbal directions, they can also follow directions by watching others (they love to copy or imitate) or in response to games or music.

As a 4-year-old's vocabulary expands, he or she will use words and sentences heard on the radio, on TV, or in their environment (home, preschool, etc.). Most children will love to recite words, phrases, and nursery rhymes at this age. Puppets are a good medium for children—especially the shy ones—to practice new words.

Math and reading concepts really begin to develop in the fourth year. A child should be able to recognize numbers and letters, as well as his or her own first name when it is printed.

Age five

At age 5, large muscle development continues. These children can coordinate their hands together for crafts such as finger painting and modeling clay. They can work with other children while making a craft. In addition, they will have become more independent, showing an interest in tying shoes and doing other tasks themselves.

Small muscle development also expands. Five-year-olds can hold crayons or pencils with ease, and they like to draw and do other pencil-and-paper activities, such as copying, tracing, coloring in pictures, and following the dots.

At age 5, most children can control body parts at will. They have a definite hand preference (right or left), and know the difference between and can respond to right/left directions.

Five-year-olds can recite simple poems and rhymes, say the letters of the alphabet in order, and can remember the sequence or pattern of riddles, games, and dance routines. Five-year-olds can respond to directions to draw a circle, square, or cross. They like directions that require them to think (such as the game Simple Simon), and they can even respond to simple written directions, such as STOP and GO.

By the age of 5, a child's math and reading skills will have developed to the point that he or she can:
- count by two to 20
- read simple commands, such as STOP and GO
- read labels printed on supplies (such as paste, glue, paint)
- recognize favorite brands of cereals and other foods

The skill chart on page xvi shows the skills developed or practiced when making each craft in this book.

To the group leaders

In any situation, but perhaps especially when dealing with preschoolers, good planning prevents big disasters. Of course, this is particularly true if you will be working with not one or two preschoolers, but an entire roomful. Groups (and their leaders) will have a much smoother and enjoyable craft time if a little planning is done first. Take the time to think about what you want the children to accomplish and what could possibly go wrong, and you'll be better prepared to face the task ahead. The following are some steps you should take for each craft you do with a group.

1. *Pick an appropriate craft.* Every craft is designed for non-reading preschoolers—who have short attention spans and lots of energy, and who probably won't be able to finish complicated or intricate projects. Many preschoolers have not yet learned how to work in a group, so don't expect things like waiting quietly in line or raising a hand to ask a question.

   Each craft is rated for cost, time to complete, adult supervision or preparation, suitability for a group, and messiness. Be sure to select a craft suitable to your group's age, abilities, and the facilities you have available. For example, if you're teaching a Sunday School class, you'll want to stay away from activities like painting, which will be too messy for children to do in their good clothes.

2. *Make the project yourself first.* This not only makes sure you fully understand the directions well enough to explain them to a roomful of eager preschoolers, it also ensures you have all the materials you need. (Be sure to include things that aren't listed in the materials/tools lists, such as paper towels and a waste basket.)

Your completed craft will serve as a model for the children, providing motivation to complete the craft. It will also help the children visualize the directions.

3. *Decide what level of order you are trying to maintain.* This is especially important if you are sharing leadership duties with another adult. Set rules of behavior before you start your project. You might even want to read these aloud and establish them as outright no-no's before you hand out craft materials. The children can be more creative when rules of behavior have been established; then they don't have to spend time testing the boundaries.

4. *Plan your clean-up just as carefully as you planned your craft.* If time is short, begin clean-up before the end of the period. You might want to set a bell timer to signal time to stop work and begin clean-up. Assign clean-up tasks to all children equally, not just to the fastest workers. Thank each child for a good job on clean-up.

5. *Plan beforehand a policy on unfinished work.* Can the child work on the project later or take it home to finish? Plan where finished and unfinished projects can be safely stored until parents come to collect their children. Be sure all children have their names on their crafts.

Skill Chart

	Page	Large muscle	Fine muscle	Eye/hand coordination	Memory sequence	Following directions	Left, right	Language development	Reading	Math
1. Play dough	2	•								
2. Macaroni beads & necklaces	4		•	•	•	•		•		
3. Book marks	6		•	•	•					
4. Feel-it pictures	8		•	•	•	•		•		
5. Help-me-set-the-table place mats	10		•	•	•	•	•			
6. Paper chain art	12		•	•	•	•	•			
7. Fun collage	14		•	•			•	•		
8. Bean bag fun	16	•	•	•	•	•	•	•		•
9. Stuffed fish & other animals	18	•	•	•		•	•			
10. Egg carton projects	20		•	•	•	•				
11. Jack-in-the-box	24		•	•	•	•		•		
12. Measuring tree	26	•		•	•	•		•		•
13. Potato faces	28		•	•	•	•		•		
14. From patterns to faces	30		•	•	•	•	•	•		
15. Look at me	32	•	•	•	•	•	•	•		
16. Changing faces	34		•	•	•	•	•			
17. Wild bird feeder	38		•	•	•	•				

Reading } Readiness · Math } Readiness

Skill Chart

#	Title	Page	Large muscle	Fine muscle	Eye/hand coordination	Memory sequence	Following directions	Left, right	Language development	Reading	Math (Readiness)
18.	Let's watch it grow	40	●	●		●		●	●		
19.	Pussywillow/popcorn picture	42	●	●	●			●			
20.	Pretty leaves to save	44	●	●	●			●			
21.	Sock puppets	48	●	●		●	●	●	●		
22.	Sack puppets	50	●	●		●	●	●	●		
23.	Puppets in a cup	52	●	●		●		●	●		
24.	Finger puppets	54	●	●		●		●	●		
25.	Valentine's Day bouquet	58	●	●				●			
26.	Egg characters for Easter	60	●	●		●		●			
27.	Mother's Day flowers	62	●	●		●		●	●		
28.	Father's Day pocket card	64	●	●		●		●	●		
29.	Independence Day collage	66	●	●		●		●			
30.	Pumpkins on parade	68	●	●		●	●	●			
31.	Thanksgiving turkeys	70	●	●		●	●	●			
32.	Pine cone people	74	●	●		●	●				
33.	String paintings Christmas wrap	76	●	●		●					
34.	Christmas ornaments	78	●	●		●		●			

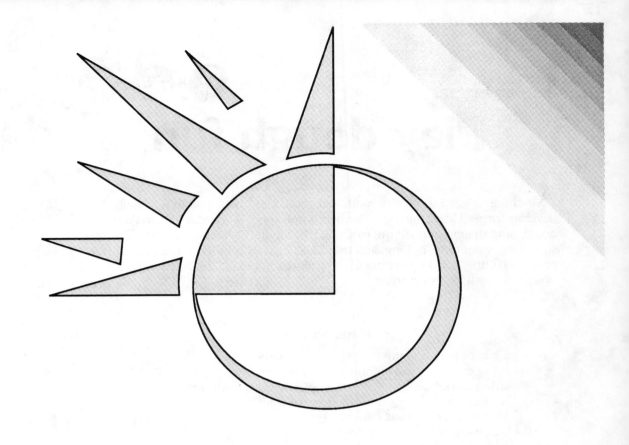

Things to do

Ages 3 and up

Play dough fun

All children need to play in mud, wet sand, clay, or play dough to help them develop arm and hand muscles. The hands must both work together, to flatten the dough, and then in opposition, to shape the dough. The experience the child has squeezing, pounding, poking, and rolling is far more important than the finished project. For this reason, encourage the children to pound, poke, pat, and roll the dough as much as they want.

Materials & tools

a ball of play dough,*
   ($1/2$ cup is a good amount)
string or ribbon
rolling pin
assortment of cookie cutters
*see recipe on following page

wax paper
straws
plastic bowl with small amount
   of flour

1. Roll the dough with the rolling pin, pressing very hard to make the dough very thin.
2. Choose a cookie cutter and press down very hard until the cutter goes all the way through the dough.
3. Lift the cookie cutter up. If the dough sticks to the cookie cutter, shake the cutter until the dough falls out.
4. Put the "fun shapes" on a piece of wax paper to dry. Push a straw through the top to make a neat hole about $1/2$ inch from the edge. The play dough will take about 2 days to dry.
5. When the play dough shape is dry, paint it, if desired. Run a string or ribbon through the hole, so the children can hang it up or wear it as a necklace.
6. With the pieces left from making the fun shapes, let the children roll a long snake, form a basket, or pinch a pretty design.

I learned . . .

I learned how to make play dough.
I learned how to use a rolling pin.
I learned how to use a cookie cutter.

Recipe for play dough using cornstarch or flour

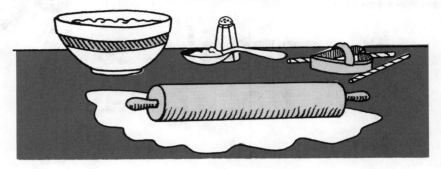

3/4	cup flour or cornstarch
3/4	cup salt
2	teaspoons powdered alum
2	teaspoons vegetable oil
	or 2 drops dish detergent
3/4	cup boiling water

This recipe is a good one to use for making fun shapes because it hardens easily. Combine flour, salt, and alum in a saucepan. Cooking over low heat, slowly add water, stirring constantly. (A double boiler will help prevent scorching.) Stir until the mixture becomes rubbery. Add vegetable oil or two drops of detergent. Stir again until well blended. Turn onto wax paper or a plate to cool. Makes enough for four large balls of play dough.

After shaping the play dough, dry it in an oven at 200° F., or let dry at room temperature for about four days. If made with cornstarch, allow the play dough to air-dry.

Macaroni beads & necklaces

Four-year-olds can do this craft if rigatoni, mostaccioli, or ziti are used. These macaroni products are about 1/4 inch in diameter, so stringing them is much easier.

You can color the macaroni with felt-tip markers or, for a softer color, with food coloring or water colors. You can even leave some of the macaroni its natural color.

Be careful not to soak the macaroni until it is soft. Spray the "beads" with hair spray to keep the color from rubbing off.

Stringing macaroni requires the use of both large and small muscles. Pushing the end of the string through the hole in the macaroni requires eye/hand coordination. For children who have trouble pushing the string through the hole in the macaroni, stiffen the end of the ribbon with glue. You might want to first tie a knot in one end of the ribbon followed by a button to prevent the beads from sliding off the end.

Materials & tools

6 pieces salad macaroni
5 pieces large size macaroni
narrow ribbon, waxed string, or
  plastic lacing

paint brushes or felt-tip markers
poster paint, food coloring, or
  watercolors

1. Count five pieces of elbow macaroni and string them on dental floss.
2. Tie the ends of the thread together so the beads won't slide off.
3. Dip the string of macaroni in the paint, and pull it out quickly. Hang the beads up to dry. The beads will need to dry for at least an hour.
4. String the six salad macaroni beads on dental floss and dip them into another color of paint. Hang them up to dry, too. Don't let them bang against the other macaroni beads. When the beads are dry, take both sets off their strings.
5. String the macaroni beads again on narrow ribbon or plastic lacing, making a pattern. Push the ribbon through the hole in the salad bead, then an elbow bead, then another salad bead. Do this until all your beads have been strung.
6. Tie the ribbon in a knot. Leave the ribbon long enough to fit over your head.

I learned . . .

I learned about different sizes of macaroni.
I learned how to string macaroni beads.
I learned how to follow a pattern to make a necklace.

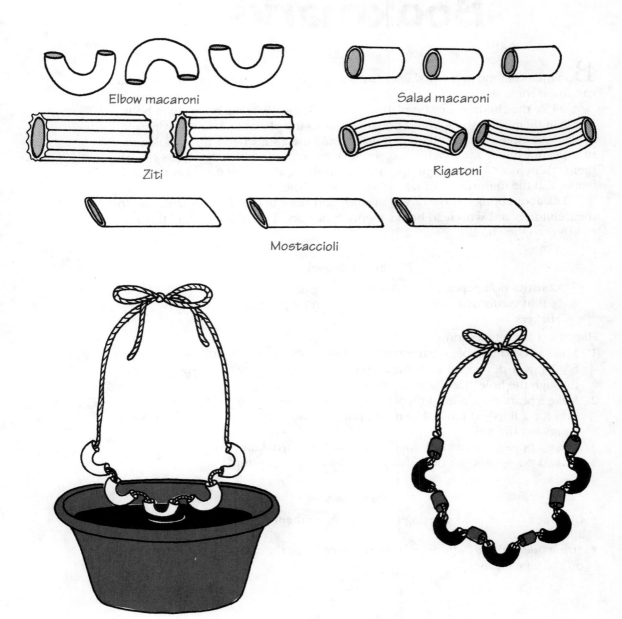

Elbow macaroni

Salad macaroni

Ziti

Rigatoni

Mostaccioli

3 Ages 3 and up

Bookmarks

Bookmarks come in many shapes, sizes and materials. Even a very young child can make some of these.

While the children are completing their craft, display some books with bookmarks in them. Talk about how a bookmark saves the place in a book. Play a game of silly questions. Ask the children if they would use a strawberry for a bookmark, or a peanut butter sandwich. Children love to respond with a loud "NO!" Ask them "Why not?" Give them opportunity to think about the function of bookmarks and the importance of taking good care of their books.

Talk about books. Show how you enjoy and value books. Parents who read to their children and who read books themselves place a value on reading that carries over to the child.

Materials & tools

construction paper, cloth ribbon, or
   thin cardboard
stickers

glue
felt-tip markers or crayons

Here are a few suggestions:

1. Make a bookmark of construction paper or a piece of thin cardboard cut 2" × 6". Draw a design on it. Poke a hole in the top and thread yarn or ribbon through the hole. Tie the yarn in a knot.
2. Make a heart-shaped bookmark out of colored paper or cloth. Add yarn or ribbon for a finished look. When you put the bookmark in a book, the ribbon hangs out the top.
3. Make a bookmark out of folded paper. Decorate front and inside.
4. Make a bookmark out of wide ribbon. Put a sticker on top.

Variations

- Cut out parts of used greeting cards and paste them on construction paper or add a ribbon to the top.
- String one to three buttons on a pipe cleaner. Twist the ends to keep the buttons on the pipe cleaner.

I learned . . .

I learned how bookmarks are used.
I learned how to make a bookmark.
I learned how to decorate a bookmark.

4

Ages 3 and up

Feel-it pictures

As soon as children pick up a crayon and make their first trial scribbles, they are ready to make feel-it pictures. With a few simple materials, children can make, paste, and feel this kind of picture.

Feel-it pictures are simple to do, and they are an excellent way to help children use the sense of touch in a new way. In addition, feel-it pictures often provide a child with his or her first experience with structured pictures.

Keep in mind that drawing around the pattern requires fine muscle skill, which will be difficult for a 3-year-old to do. Be sure to accept the children's drawings without corrections or negative comments.

Talk about the picture. If the children want to tell you a story about their pictures, write down what they dictate, and read it back to them. Then have each child "read" it back to you.

Materials & tools

1 large piece of construction paper or
   newsprint
scissors
glue

cotton
crayons, paint, or felt-tip markers
patterns of rabbits or sheep

1. Trace around the picture of the animal onto the construction paper, using a crayon, paint, or a felt-tip marker.
2. Find the part of the animal that looks like cotton, and glue some cotton on that part until the animal looks soft and fuzzy.

Variations

- Draw a picture of something soft and fluffy, and glue the cotton onto the soft and fluffy parts.
- Use other types of materials—such as felt, velvet, corduroy, feathers, leather, or sandpaper—to give the child other experiences touching and feeling.

I learned . . .

I learned how to make a picture I can feel.
I learned that cotton is soft.
I learned the names of some soft and fuzzy animals.

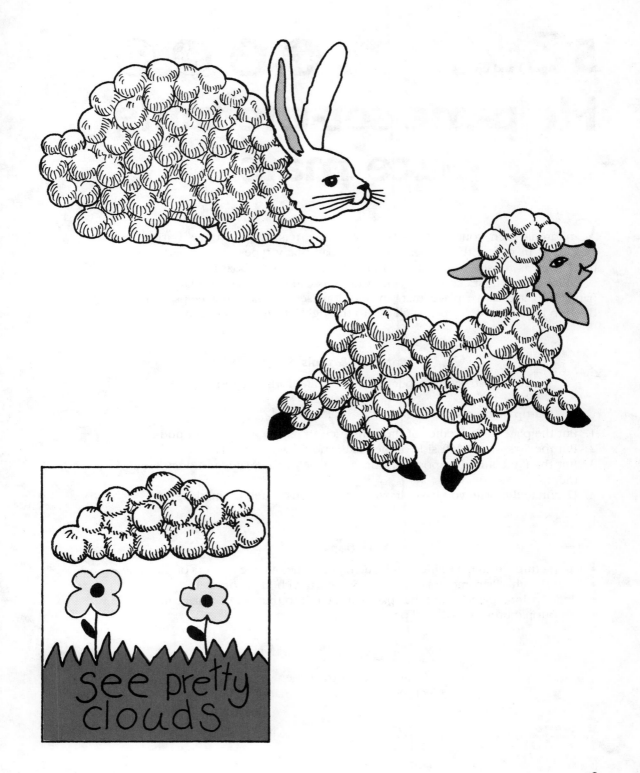

see pretty
clouds

9

5 Ages 3 and up

Help-me-set-the-table place mats

Children—even young ones—can make place mats several times during the year to fit in with a theme, season, or holiday. Many types of materials can be used, such as construction paper, cardboard, cloth, poster board, or plastic.

Ribbon, yarn, stickers, and cutout designs can change an ordinary piece of paper into a creative place mat. In addition, setting the table helps children develop important concepts, such as "to the right of" and "between."

Materials & tools

1 piece construction paper, 12" × 18"
felt-tip markers or crayons
plate, knife, fork, & spoon to use as patterns

1. Put the plate in the center of the construction paper, and draw around it.
2. Put the fork on the left side of the plate, and draw around it.
3. Put the knife and the spoon on the right side of the plate, and draw around them.
4. Decorate the plate you have drawn using crayons or felt-tip markers.

Variations

- Cut pictures from magazines, and glue them in the outside corners of the paper
- Print the child's name in large letters & have the child decorate it
- Finger-paint a piece of butcher paper and cut it to the size of a place mat
- Cut out pictures of food and paste them on the mat

I learned . . .

I learned to set the table.
I learned to make a place mat.

Paper chain art

Paper chains are inexpensive to make and a good way to use scraps of paper.

Cut paper strips about 5" long and 1" wide. Select strips of colors that go with a season or a theme: for example, make a chain of orange and black for Halloween or red and green for Christmas. (Christmas wrapping paper also makes an interesting paper chain.)

Put the strips in piles according to colors for the children to use. For younger children, you might want to hold each loop with a paper clip until the glue dries.

Materials & tools

an assortment of strips of colored
paper, cut into 5"-×-1" strips   glue

1. Make a loop of a paper strip. Put some glue on the outside of one end of the strip and press the two ends together until the glue holds.
2. Take a second paper strip, and put it through the first loop. Make a loop out of it, and paste it together just like you did with the first loop. Now you have made the first link in a chain.
3. Continue making links in the chain. You can make the chain as long as you want.
4. If you like, you can make a picture that will help you count the days until Christmas. Make a Christmas picture, and put a chain with 25 loops on the picture. Each day, cut off one of the loops and count the ones left to find out how many days until Christmas. You can even make a jingle about it (see illustration).

Variations

* At a day camp, children made paper chains into a flag of the United States and pasted stars on it for the Fourth of July.
* Teachers frequently use chains to decorate the room. After a verse or a vocabulary word is mastered it can be added as a link to the chain. Soon the chain stretches from wall to wall.
* To decorate a miniature Christmas tree or an Easter egg tree, make the strips shorter and narrower.

I learned . . .

I learned how to paste a strip of paper into a loop.
I learned how to link the loops together.
I learned how to follow a pattern.

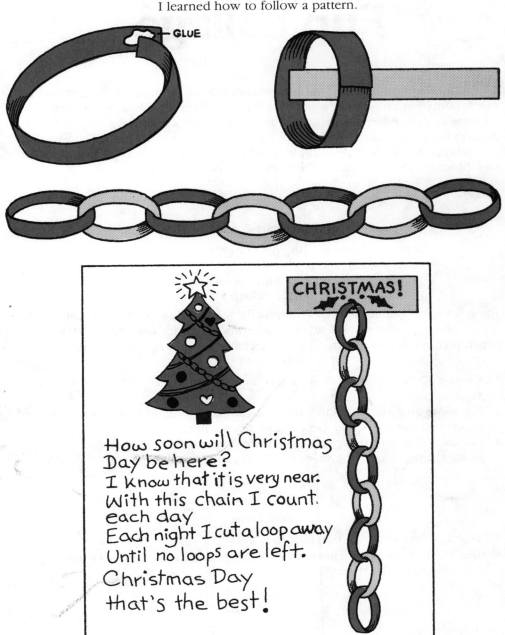

GLUE

CHRISTMAS!

How soon will Christmas
Day be here?
I know that it is very near.
With this chain I count
each day
Each night I cut a loop away
Until no loops are left.
Christmas Day
that's the best!

7 Ages 3 and up

Fun collage

Making a collage is a task most children can do all by themselves. Discuss the word *collage* with the children and have them say it several times. No two collages are ever exactly alike. Be careful not to compare the children's work or to ask them to copy your model.

Making a collage helps children develop concepts about things that go together and aids in increasing their attention spans.

Materials & tools

1 piece of construction paper or thin
    cardboard, about 4″ × 6″
an assortment of items with interesting
    shapes or textures (see below)

glue
scissors

Some ideas for collage items: pebbles, shells, seeds, twigs, dry moss, small leaves, dried flowers, pine needles, feathers, macaroni, salt, sand, small pieces of colored paper, pictures cut from magazines or greeting cards, strips of computer paper holes, foil, colored tissue paper, or colored plastic wrap

1. Choose several different objects (no more than four, to start with) to use in your collage.
2. Put some glue on your sheet of paper or cardboard, and place some of the objects on the glue spots. Let the glue dry a while.
3. Put more glue on the paper, and sprinkle some sand or salt on top of the glue. Shake the paper over the waste basket to get rid of all the extra salt or sand.

Variations

- Make a collage in a shoe box lid.
- Make a collage using a theme with such things as dried flowers, sea shells, types of macaroni, seeds, or beans.

I learned . . .

I learned what the word *collage* means.
I learned how to make a collage.
I learned that some things feel different than others.

8 Ages 4 and up

Beanbag fun

This craft requires the adult to make the beanbag for the child to fill and decorate. Some sewing with the machine can be done with one child at a time, but be sure there is someone else available to supervise the other children.

Older children can measure the beans or rice to be put into each bag, filling the bags while the leader stitches them shut. Younger children can decorate the completed beanbags.

The value of making beanbags goes far beyond the construction project. For example, throwing and catching are necessary to the development of basic perception, and children can catch a beanbag much easier than they can a ball: A beanbag will not roll, and it conforms to the shape of the hand. Following the path of a tossed beanbag increases a short attention span, and a group game of toss-and-catch teaches the important social skill of ''waiting your turn.''

One final note: When the beanbags get dirty, throw them away. Washing them only makes bean soup!

Materials & tools

1 piece of heavy cotton or felt cloth
  16″ × 6″, (or 2 pieces, 8″ × 6″)
about 1 cup dry beans or rice
sewing machine

needle & thread
scissors
measuring cup

1. If you are using one piece of cloth, fold it in half to make an 8″ × 6″ rectangle. If you are using two pieces of cloth, place them together, wrong sides together.
2. Stitch around three sides of the rectangle, about 1/2″ from the edges. Leave the top open.
3. Fill the bag with about one cup of beans or rice. Push all the beans toward the bottom.
4. Stitch across the open top. If your machine has a zig-zag stitch, go around all the sides again for a sturdier finish. (With one-to-one adult supervision, a child can stitch across the bean bag on the machine after an adult has basted it.)

Variation

• Cut a hole in the middle of a cardboard box, and use it as a target for throwing the beanbags. Make the game even more fun by cutting different sized holes or by drawing a face on the box with holes for the eyes, nose, and mouth (see illustration).

I learned . . .

I learned what dry beans look like.
I learned how to measure with a measuring cup.
I learned how to throw beanbags at a target.

Leave open to fill with beans!

Shapes for bean bags

9

Ages 3 and up

Stuffed fish
& other animals

This craft can be made to carry out a theme or as a decoration for a party. Because the paint needs to be completely dry before stapling and drawing on the paper, the project will take more than one session to complete. You can complete the project in about 20 minutes using crayons or felt-tip markers, but I recommend providing the child with the freedom of movement and creativity of paints or finger paints.

This craft can be filled with candy treats to make the piñata game played by children in Mexico. Hang the piñata in the center of a circle. One by one, blindfold the children and let them take turns trying to break open the fish with a stick so that the candy will spill out.

Materials & tools

2 large sheets of butcher paper
newspaper, torn into strips for stuffing
stapler (for the adult to use)

crayons, markers, paints and
  brushes, or finger paints

1. Decorate two sheets of butcher paper with finger paints, paints and brushes, crayons, or felt-tip markers. Allow the design to dry.
2. When the paper is dry, draw a large fish on one paper. Cut it out. Turn it over and trace around it to draw a fish on the other paper. Before you cut the second fish out, check to see that the two fish face each other.
3. Cut around the second fish.
4. Put the two fish together, and staple around the outside. Leave a space at the top of the fish to stuff with newspaper (or candy, if you're making a piñata).
5. Draw one eye and half a mouth on each side of the fish. Then stuff your fish with wadded newspaper.
6. Staple a string on your fish so you can hang it up to make a decoration for a party or your room.

Variations

- Draw and cut out other animals such as: rabbits for Easter, turkeys for Thanksgiving, pumpkins for Halloween, frogs or turtles, teddy bears.

I learned . . .

I learned how to make a stuffed fish.
I learned how to make the left side different from the right side.
I learned what a fish looks like from the side.

Leave open to stuff with newspaper

10 Ages 5 and up

Egg carton projects

Making flowers and other objects out of egg cartons requires a child to visualize changes that take place as the craft is constructed from the raw materials. Display the pot of flowers you made as a model to help the children visualize what they are going to make.

The children might need help cutting the egg carton. They will also need help pushing the stem into the flower and the cardboard circle. If the pot of flowers tips over, put something heavy, like a marble, in the paper cup.

Making a pot of egg carton flowers helps the children practice eye/hand coordination by cutting and drawing around the flower pot and by stringing the beads on the pipe cleaners, and it expands their vocabularies to include the parts of a flower (stem, petal, etc.).

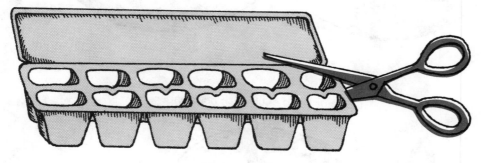

Materials & tools

egg cartons	paint brushes
(cardboard or Styrofoam)	paper cups or small clay pots
pipe cleaners	cardboard circles
scissors	poster paint
glue	small buttons or beads

1. Cut each egg cup apart. Cut a V in the middle of each side of egg cup to form flower petals as in a tulip.
2. If you have cardboard egg cartons, paint the egg cups, inside and out (any color), and let them dry. Styrofoam egg cartons, on the other hand, are difficult to paint. If you don't like the color of the Styrofoam egg carton, try adding powdered cleanser to the poster paint to get it to coat the egg cups.
3. Put a bead or button on one end of a pipe cleaner stem. Bend the pipe cleaner so the bead will not fall off.

4. When the egg cups are dry, push the other end of the pipe cleaner through the bottom of the egg cup. The bead will stop it from going through all the way. Now you have a flower on a stem.
5. Turn the flower pot or paper cup upside-down on a piece of cardboard. Draw around it, and cut out the shape.
6. Push the stem ends of pipe cleaners through the cardboard circle.
7. Place the cardboard circle in the paper cup or clay pot. You now have a pot of flowers to use on the table. A pretty ribbon tied around the flower pot will add color.

Cut here

I learned . . .

I learned some other uses for egg cartons.
I learned the words *petal* and *stem*.
I learned how to make a decoration for the table.

Variations

- Make flowers to hang on a mobile.
- Make bookworms by cutting the egg cups apart and stringing them together.
- Make flowers on stems and tie them together with ribbon to make a corsage.

Learning about me

Jack-in-the-box

Children love things that move. Demonstrate how to put the jack-in-the-box into the berry box so that the head doesn't catch on the side of the box. Some 4-year-old children might be able to fold the strips over to make the spring after an adult demonstrates; some might need more help.

This craft helps children follow a demonstration, learn to fold, and experiment with language by making up a jingle.

Materials & tools

2 colors of construction paper,
   cut into 2"-×-24" strips
   (for the spring)
1 3"-×-6" piece white paper
   (for the head)
1 berry box
glue

pencil
scissors
crayons or felt-tip pens
1 4"-×-4" cardboard square
   (for the lid)
tape for hinge

1. Choose two strips of paper in two different colors.
2. Turn one strip up. Turn the other strip sideways over the first one.
3. Fold the first strip over the second one. Fold the second one over the first one. Keep doing this until you have used all the strips.
4. Make a head for your jack-in-the-box by folding the white paper in half. With the fold at the top, draw a face on the paper and color it. Then cut around the head, being sure to keep the fold at the top.
5. Fold and paste the front neck to the back one. Paste the neck to the spring.
6. Make a design on the lid of the box. Tape it to one edge of the box, and put Jack into the box, spring first.
7. Make up a jingle about your jack-in-the-box, or memorize this one:

> Jack is quiet down in his box
> Until someone opens the lid
> And UP he POPS!

Variations

- Use a paper cup with a lid
- Use a paper milk carton and make a lid
- Use a salt box or oatmeal box cut in half
- Use a small size coffee can, or nut can. Cover the metal can with paper.

I learned . . .

I learned how to make a spring by folding paper.
I learned a jingle about Jack-in-the-box.

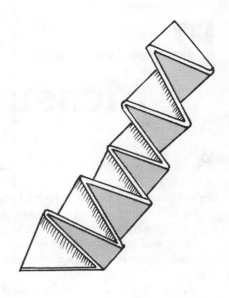

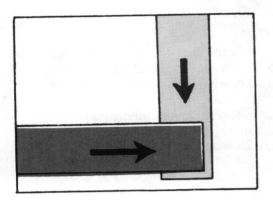

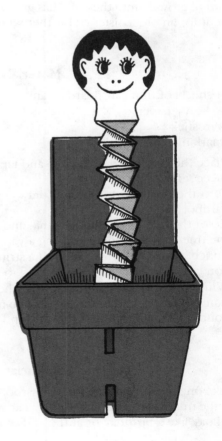

12 Ages 3 and up

Measuring tree

A model will help the child visualize how the cardboard becomes a measuring tree. Be sure the concept of a tall tree trunk is understood. The child will need supervision to tape the cardboard together. Make sure it doesn't come apart or slip when you turn the long strip over.

Talk about how the tree will keep a record of how much the child grows. The children will not only develop a positive self-image by using their measuring tree to mark their growth, they will also begin to understand the concept of measuring.

This craft gives the child something to take home. It can be used to keep a record of growth until the child has grown into an adult, and it makes an excellent present for an older sister or brother when a new baby comes home.

Materials & tools

4 sheets of thin cardboard or any
   heavy paper, 6″ × 12″
yardstick
marking pens

masking tape or shipping tape
hole punch (for the leader to use)
string

1. Place the cardboard on a table and tape the pieces together to make one long piece 4 feet long.
2. Turn the cardboard over, and draw a tree from the bottom to the top of the cardboard.
3. Color the tree. Make a long trunk, and put some leaves on the top. Then mark the tree in inches and feet using a yardstick.
4. Punch a hole at the top, and put a string through it. Tie a knot in the string so you can hang up your tree. Be sure to put your name at the top of the tree.
5. With your tree hanging up so that the bottom of the tree touches the floor, stand against the tree. Have someone put a mark on the tree where the top of your head touches it. Put the date and your age next to the mark on the tree.

Variations

- Make one measuring tree for a classroom of children. Mark each child's height on the tree at the beginning of the year. Mark each child's height again on a special day like a birthday or at the end of the year.

I learned . . .

I learned about measuring.
I learned how tall I am.
I learned what a yardstick is used for.

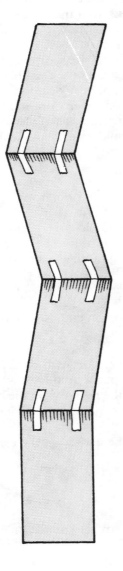

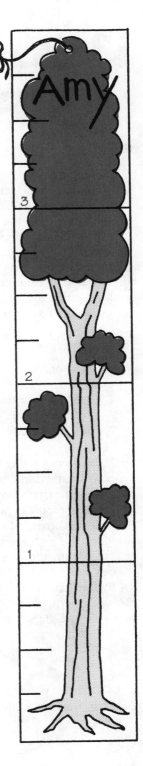

13 Ages 4 and up

Potato faces

Making a potato face provides an opportunity to talk about potatoes, how they grow underground, and that new potato plants sprout from the eyes. If possible, bring in an old potato that has started to sprout. Show the children how the sprouts start from the eyes.

You need to draw the parts of the face on a sheet of construction paper beforehand, so the children can color and cut them out. The children will need help cutting out the glasses. Make a pattern out of heavy cardboard for the children to draw around, or make copies using carbon paper. Copies can also be made by blackening the back side of the original with pencil. Then place it over a clean sheet of paper and trace over the shapes. The children can help with this activity.

Materials & tools

a large potato
construction paper for a hat
2"-×-5" strip of thin cardboard or a
   bathroom tissue or paper towel roll
   cut into 2-inch sections
scissors

felt-tips or crayons
glue
toothpicks
patterns for: 2 ears, 2 eyes, nose,
   mouth, glasses

1. Make a neck using the bathroom tissue or paper towel roll or a strip of cardboard curved into a tube.
2. Put your potato on the ring so it will stand up on end. Now you are ready to put a face on the potato.
3. Color the parts of the face, and cut them out.
4. Place the paper eyes on the potato. Stick them on with toothpicks. Do the same with the nose and the mouth. Next, put a toothpick where each ear belongs, and put on the ears. Be sure to put the right ear on the right side and the left ear on the left. When you have the parts of the face just where you want them, glue them in place.
5. Color the glasses and cut them out. Fasten the glasses on the ears. Make sure the potato can see through the glasses!

Variations

- Use a paper plate instead of a potato
- Use a round box such as an oatmeal box, salt box, or coffee can. Cover the can with paper and glue on the facial parts.

I learned . . .

I learned that potatoes have eyes but can't see.
I learned that new potatos grow from potato eyes.
I learned that potatoes grow underground.

Potato plant

How potatoes grow underground

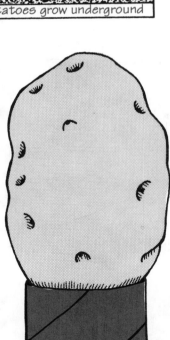

14

Ages 4 and up

From patterns to faces

A 3-year-old can make this craft if the child has plenty of supervision. Be sure the children put none of the objects in their mouths. **NOTE:** For younger children, this project could present a choking hazard, so be sure to choose very large buttons.

This craft gives an opportunity to practice right and left and to learn more about facial features. Besides the fun the children will have completing a funny face, they will also learn the shape of eyes, ears, nose, and mouth, and they will learn to visualize the parts of the face as they glue them on the plate.

The carrot will stick with any type of liquid glue. In a few days the carrot pieces will shrink into a long thin wrinkled nose. The children will enjoy seeing the change that takes place.

Materials & tools

1 paper plate, (dessert or 9-inch size)	2 pieces of cardboard for ears
2 buttons for eyes	scissors
1 larger button for nose	glue
red felt or yarn for mouth	pencil
1 piece of ribbon for tie	felt-tip markers or crayons

1. Place two buttons near the top of the plate to make the eyes, and a button in the center of the plate to make a nose.
2. Once you have the buttons where you want them, glue all three buttons in place.
3. Make a yarn or felt mouth. Glue it on the plate.
4. Draw two ears on a piece of cardboard. Cut them out. Glue them on the plate.
5. Add a bow tie made of ribbon or make a paper one and decorate it. Glue it to the bottom of the plate.

Variations

- Instead of buttons for eyes, use slices of carrots.
- Glue a brown bean in the center of each eye.
- Use the end of the carrot for a long, pointed nose.

I learned . . .

I learned to name the parts of a face.
I learned about left and right.
I learned that carrots shrink as they dry.

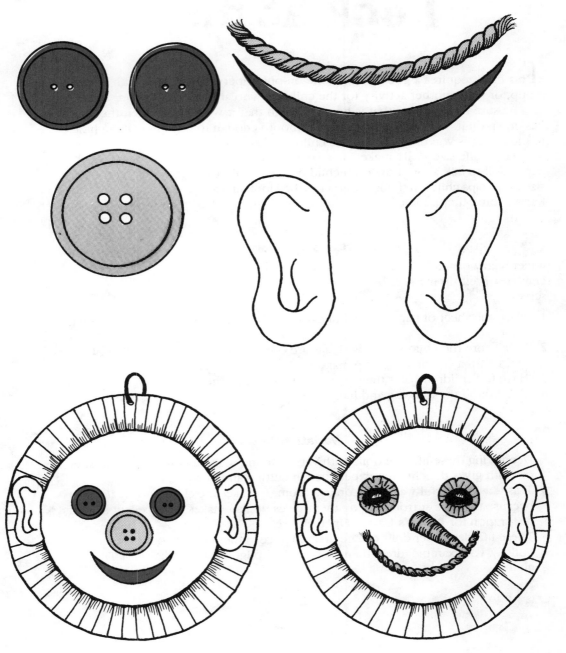

15

Ages 4 and up

Look at me

This craft requires a good deal of one-on-one supervision. Use it with a small group, or plan another activity for the children who are waiting for their turn.

Be sure to use paper that is heavy enough that it won't tear when the child lies down on it. Also be sure the floor is smooth enough to prevent making holes in the paper as you draw around the child.

These life-size dolls make interesting room decorations. You can use the paper doll to talk about how each child has his or her own size. Making the life-size doll helps children think about what they look like and what makes them different from other people.

Materials & tools

4 feet heavy paper
crayons or felt-tip markers
scissors

1. Place the sheet of paper on the uncarpeted floor, and have the child lie down on it.
2. Being sure the child's arms and legs are on the paper, draw an outline of the child with a crayon or felt-tip marker.
3. Have the children color their drawings to look like they do.
4. Cut around the drawing and hang it up.

Variations

- Decorating these life-size dolls with yarn hair and making clothes of wallpaper or cloth gives the children experience in cutting and decorating.
- This is a wonderful way to decorate a room. It makes the children feel at home because they are surrounded by themselves. It also makes an excellent school decoration for Parent's Day or Open House.
- These life-size paper dolls can be dressed in costumes to carry out a theme or a holiday. For example, dress them to represent pilgrims and Indians for Thanksgiving.

I learned . . .

I learned how tall I am.
I learned how to look at myself carefully.
I learned how to cut around a big figure.

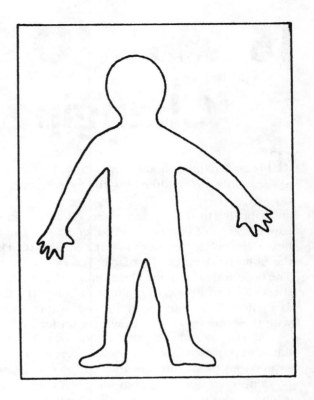

16 Ages 4 and up

Changing faces

This craft requires adult preparation. Be sure to make a model for the children to see. Show the children how the face changes as you flip up different combinations.

Drawing the four different faces is easy even if you are not artistic. Use typing paper instead of construction paper, so you can trace each face as you draw the next. First divide the paper in three equal parts. Draw a dotted line from the top to the bottom. Draw the first face. The eyes must be on the two outside sections. The nose and mouth must be entirely within the middle section. Place the second sheet of paper on top of the first and draw the facial features using the first sheet as a guide. Try to put the eyes, nose, and mouth in the same place. Do the same with the other two faces. Draw one set for each child, or photocopy one set.

As you lay out the faces before the children, ask them to find the sad face, then the surprised face, the sleepy face, and the happy face. Talk about what facial expressions mean and how they add to our ability to communicate.

This craft helps children understand how our faces show how we feel, and teaches them how to discriminate between those feelings. By turning different strips of the paper face, the child can experiment with different expressions.

Materials & tools

1 sheet of construction paper, 9″ × 12″	crayons or felt-tip markers
4 sheets of paper with a different face drawn on each (see drawing)	clear tape
	scissors
	glue

1. Color the eyes, nose, and mouth on each of the four faces.
2. Tape the sad face on the construction paper. Use three pieces of tape. Put one piece of tape at the top between the dotted lines and one on either side. This will make a hinge when the faces are cut on the dotted lines.
3. Tape the surprised face on top of the sad face. Use three pieces of tape the same way as you did the sad face. The tape for the hinges can go on top of each other.
4. Tape the sleepy face on top of the surprised face. Use three pieces of tape in the same way.
5. The happy face goes on top of the sleepy face. Tape it the same way.
6. See the dotted lines on each of the faces. Cut on these lines from the bottom to the top of the paper. Do the same with all the other faces.

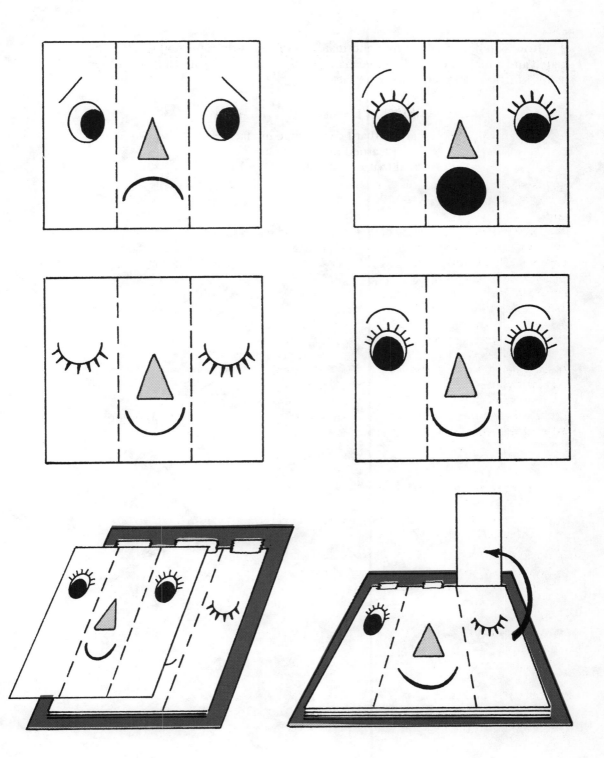

Now you have faces to mix and match. Turn the strips and see which parts match and which ones don't. You can make part of the face smile while the other half is sad. You can even make your face wink.

I learned . . .

I learned that I can change my face.
I learned how to wink.
I learned that my face shows how I feel.

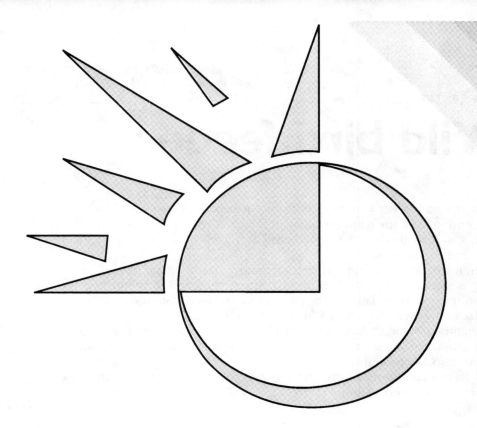

Things around me

17 Ages 4 and up

Wild bird feeder

Making a bird feeder gives you an opportunity to talk about wild birds and what they eat, and to learn the names of a few of the most common birds in your area. This craft will help children develop a sense of the world around them and of the need to care for animals.

The children will need help tying the string tightly around the pine cone. Be sure the string is strong enough to hold up to a strong wind and to support the weight of any birds that might land on the pine cone. The feeder should be hung from a strong branch where no cats or squirrels can reach it.

It's only natural for the children to want to taste the peanut butter, so you might want to give them some crackers with peanut butter to eat while you talk about how birds also like peanut butter.

This bird feeder can be made in almost any location and in a short time. Younger children might need an apron or an old shirt worn backwards to protect their clothing.

Materials & tools

1 large pine cone	$^{1}/_{2}$ cup of peanut butter
spoon or table knife	1 cup of bird seed
6 inches of string	wax paper

1. Cover the table where you are going to work with wax paper. Have everyone wash and dry their hands.
2. Push a spoonful of peanut butter between the petals of the pine cone. Keep doing this until you have filled all the spaces between the petals of the pine cone or used up all your peanut butter.
3. Sprinkle birdseed on the wax paper.
4. Roll the pine cone filled with peanut butter around in the birdseed. Get as many seeds as possible on the cone.
5. Tie a string at the top of the pine cone so you can hang up your pine cone bird feeder in a tree or from a fence post. Try to tie it high so cats and squirrels can't get to it. Watch and see which birds come to the pine cone to eat the seeds and peanut butter.

I learned . . .

I learned how to make a bird feeder.
I learned that seeds stick to peanut butter.
I learned that birds like peanut butter.

Fill between petals
with peanut butter

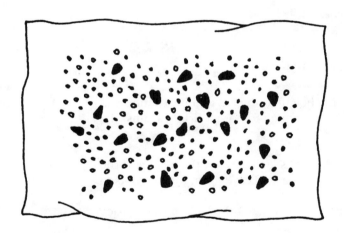

39

Let's watch it grow

This craft provides the child an opportunity to observe nature at work. It is best done where the child will have the opportunity to observe the seeds daily. Any type of beans can be used, but lima beans are the easiest to observe because of their size and shape. Use beans from a seed package rather than beans packaged for food. Beans packaged for food may have been treated to prevent sprouting.

This science craft enables children to observe how seeds grow, better understand the importance of water, learn about the time needed for germination, and expand their vocabulary with the words *sprouts, roots, stem, lima beans,* etc. It also helps them develop a sense of time: How long does it take a plant to grow?

Materials & tools

6 sheets of paper towels
1 glass jar, (pint or smaller)
4 to 6 beans (lima beans are the easiest
  to observe)

1. Fold paper towels until they are the same height as the jar. Roll into a tube and place in the jar. The tube should fill the jar enough to hold it firmly against the sides of the jar.
2. Dampen the tube of paper towels.
3. Put the seeds in the jar one by one. Put each seed between the glass and the paper towel about halfway down the side of the jar. Leave room for the roots to grow down and the stem to grow up.
4. Pour some water into the jar to keep the paper wet. Set the jar in a warm place with plenty of light.
5. Observe the seeds in the jar every day. Add water if the towel tube is dry. In a few days, the beans will sprout.

I learned . . .

I learned that beans are seeds.
I learned the words *sprout, root,* and *stem.*
I learned how long it takes a plant to grow.
I learned that plants need water to grow.

TWO WEEKS LATER...

19 Ages 3 and up

Pussy willow & popcorn pictures

You will need to have plenty of pussy willows to do this craft. Show the children how they grow on the branch. You might even want to let the children help you pick it off the branch, but be sure to tell the children that they can feel—but not taste—the pussy willow.

If pussy willows are not available in your area, make a popcorn picture. If possible, show the children what an ear of popcorn looks like. If time is limited or you wish to keep the children clean, color the popcorn yourself beforehand. You might also want to have a bowl of popcorn on hand for the children to eat before they make their pictures. While it's OK to eat colored popcorn, it probably won't taste very good since it's been wet.

Making these pictures will not only develop a child's sense of touch and texture, but it will also provide you with an opportunity to discuss how both pussy willow and popcorn start out as living plants.

Materials & tools

construction paper	glue
pencil	paper towels
pussy willow buds on branches	slotted spoon
felt-tip markers	food coloring
popcorn	

Pussy willow pictures

1. Draw a design on the construction paper
2. Decorate it with pussy willows.
3. Glue the pussy willows in place on the picture.

Popcorn painting

1. Fill medium-sized bowls with water. Add a few drops of different colors of food coloring to each bowl and mix.
2. Put a few kernels of popped corn in each bowl of colored water, and stir them around to color them. Remove the popcorn with a slotted spoon, and put it on a paper towel to dry.

3. Draw a picture of something and spread it with glue. Glue the different colors of popcorn on the paper to color the picture.

I learned . . .

I learned that pussy willows grow on branches.
I learned that popcorn comes from a plant.
I learned how to color popcorn.

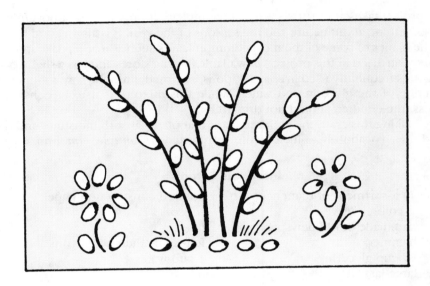

20 Ages 5 and up

Pretty leaves to save

This project takes at least two weeks to complete. It provides an opportunity to teach something about nature and the seasons of the year. It is also a good time to learn the names of some of the most common leaves such as maple, oak, and elm.

Glycerin (used in this project) is available in drug stores and has a slightly oily feeling. It is frequently used in soaps, lotions, and medicines. Be sure to supervise the mixing of the glycerin and water. While this mixture is usually considered harmless, the children should not drink it.

By making this craft, the children learn that plants absorb moisture, and they expand their vocabulary to include the words *glycerin, maple, elm, oak,* etc.

Materials & tools

an assortment of branches with colored leaves	colored construction paper
pad made of old newspapers	scissors
hammer	tape
$1/2$ cup glycerin	felt-tip markers or crayons
large jar	1 cup water
	mixing bowl

1. Put the branches of leaves on a pad of newspapers. Pound the ends of the branches with a hammer until the stems feel soft. (This helps to absorb the glycerin mixture.)
2. Mix 1 cup of water with $1/2$ cup glycerin. Put the crushed stems into the glycerin/water mixture and let them stand for 2 weeks.
3. After 2 weeks, remove the stems from the glycerin mixture, and wipe off any excess moisture. The leaves are now ready to use in an autumn arrangement.
4. Cover a tall juice can with construction paper (which can be decorated). Put the leaves in this container. The leaves will have a waxy look and will be preserved for an attractive autumn centerpiece.

I learned . . .

I learned that leaves change color in the fall.
I learned that plants absorb moisture.
I learned the words *glycerin, maple, elm, oak, autumn,* and *preserve.*

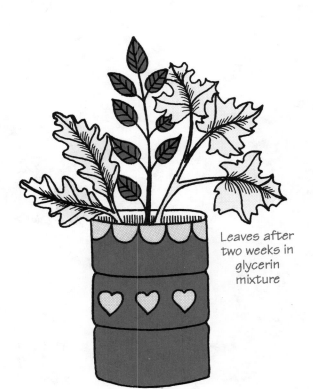

Leaves after two weeks in glycerin mixture

Puppets
I can make

21

Sock puppets

Making and playing with puppets is an excellent way for children to practice and learn language skills. Many children who are too shy to speak to peers or adults will enjoy the freedom of "talking" through a puppet.

Puppets also help children be creative as they experiment with dialects, new forms of language, and different personalities. Physically, children will develop better finger-and-thumb control through working the puppets.

Be sure to make a model for the children so they'll know exactly where to place the eyes and the duck bill of the puppet.

Materials & tools

1 white or light-colored child's sock
felt-tip markers or crayons

1. Lay the sock flat with the heel up and the top of the sock down.
2. Draw a big black eye on each side about halfway between the heel and the toe.
3. Draw a duck bill on each side of the sock starting near the eye and going down at an angle toward the toe. Color the bill orange. Do the same on the other side of the sock.
4. Put the puppet on your hand. Push the toe of the sock in to make a mouth in the bill, and move your fingers and thumb to make your puppet talk.

Variation

• Use scraps of cloth or construction paper for the eyes and duck bill.

I learned . . .

I learned how to use my fingers and thumb.
I learned how to make the puppet talk.
I learned how to make a sock puppet.

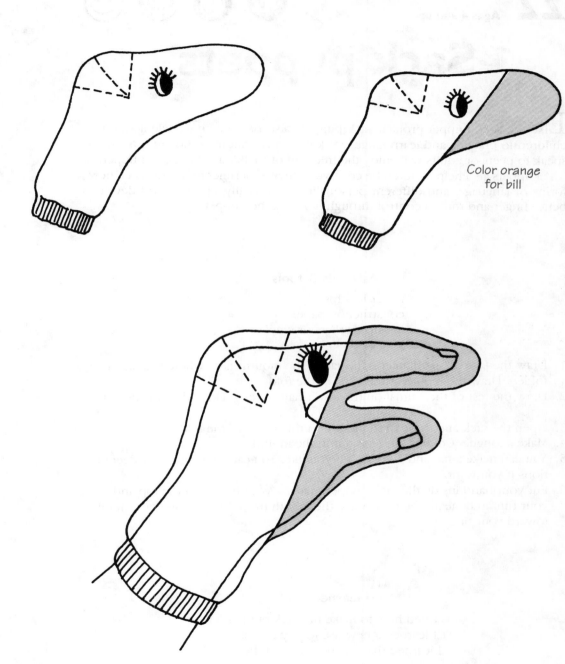

Color orange
for bill

Sack puppets

Like the sock puppet project, sack puppets also provide an excellent way for children to practice and learn language skills. Many children who are too shy to speak to peers or adults will enjoy the freedom of "talking" through a puppet.

Puppets also help children be creative as they experiment with dialects, new forms of language, and different personalities. Physically, children will develop better finger-and-thumb control through working the puppets.

Materials & tools

paper lunch sack
construction paper
felt-tip markers or crayons
glue or paste

1. Draw the face of an animal on the sack. The mouth starts where the sack is folded. Draw the mouth at the edge of the fold.
2. Draw the rest of the animal on the lower half of the sack, and color the animal.
3. Open the sack and draw a red mouth on the inside of the fold.
4. Make a tongue. Color it, and paste it in the mouth.
5. You can make a hat and glue it on if you like. You can also add other decorations if you want.
6. Put your hand inside the sack puppet, placing your fingers in the top and your thumb beneath the fold. Make the mouth move by moving your thumb toward your fingers.

I learned . . .

I learned how to make my sack puppet talk.
I learned a new use for a paper sack.
I learned that a paper sack can be fun.

23

Ages 5 and up

Puppets in a cup

Puppets in a cup are easy to make, and the children can complete the craft in a short time. The puppets also can carry out a theme, such as Halloween pumpkins or Easter rabbits.

You can help the children develop language skills by reading them rhymes and jingles (see the one at the end of this project). Have the children make up some of their own. Encourage them to experiment with their imaginations.

Children adjust to new situations easier when they can express their fear through a puppet. Shy children will respond to adult questions much easier if they let the puppet do the talking. An adult can use a puppet to explain rules of behavior or what to expect in an upcoming situation.

Materials & tools

1 section of an egg carton	tape
1 paper cup, 6 oz. size	glue
yarn or string	scissors
construction paper	felt-tip markers or crayons
straw or popsicle stick	

1. Cut out one section of an egg carton, and draw a face on it.
2. Poke a hole in the egg cup at the top, and push the straw or popsicle stick through the hole. Put a spot of glue on the straw or stick to hold it in place.
3. Use string or yarn to make hair for your puppet. Glue the hair on top of the head. You can cover the hole you just made with the hair.
4. Poke a hole in the bottom of the paper cup. Push the other end of the straw or stick through that hole.
5. Now you have a puppet in a cup. The cup is the puppet's stage. You can make your puppet turn around or peek over the side of the stage at you. He can hide and then jump up.
6. You can make up a rhyme about your puppet. I like this one.

> I am a puppet
> I live in a cup
> I can go down
> I can jump up.

I learned . . .

I learned how to make a different kind of puppet.
I learned how to make the puppet move.
I learned a rhyme about a puppet.

Yarn
for hair

24 Ages 4 and up

Finger puppets

These puppets are easy to make and can be used to carry out a theme or illustrate a lesson. They are good to make when time and supplies are limited.

These two types of puppets give children variety and good practice using their fingers. Have models to help the children visualize the finished craft and to follow the oral directions.

Through making finger puppets the children practice eye/hand coordination and finger-and-thumb movements. They can also experiment with language as they make the puppet "talk." Encourage the children to try on different personalities with different voices as they talk for the puppets—booming voice for the father, squeaky voice for the baby, etc.

Materials & tools

1 piece white construction paper,
   thin cardboard, or 3-×-5 card
scissors

glue
felt-tip markers or crayons

Finger puppets

Have models to show the children the right size to make the puppets.
1. Draw a picture of a girl or a boy or an animal. Make it the same size as the model.
2. Color the picture, and cut it out very carefully. Be sure to leave the two tabs that wrap around your finger.
3. Have someone help you wrap it around your finger and tape it.
4. Now you have a finger puppet. You can make it move when you move your finger. You can make more finger puppets and put them on other fingers of either hand. Then they can talk to each other.

Two-finger puppets

1. Trace around the puppet pattern on a piece of white construction paper.
2. Decorate each face as much as you want. Dress your puppet. You can even draw a hat or long hair on some of the puppets.
3. Cut the puppets out carefully. Ask your leader to help you cut the holes in the bottom.
4. Push two fingers of your hand through the holes. You can make your puppet walk with your fingers.

I learned . . .

I learned how to make two different kinds of puppet.
I learned how to make puppets that walk.
I learned how to cut carefully.

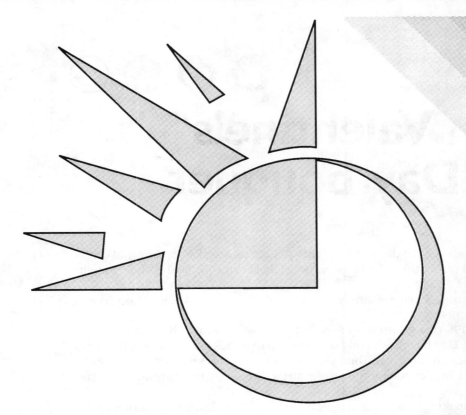

Making things
for
special days

25 Ages 3 and up

Valentine's Day bouquet

Valentines fascinate children. With plenty of materials available, the child can be very creative. Putting the valentines on popsicle sticks adds to the child's ability to hold and feel a valentine.

These valentines make a showy gift. Children love to make, give and receive valentines.

When you have a group of children, a good way for the children to receive their valentines is to have each child decorate a paper sack and put his or her name on it. The other children can then put valentines in the sacks of their friends. When the sacks are decorated, they make attractive decorations around the classroom.

Through making this valentine bouquet, children learn to practice spatial relationships (What will fit on the end of a stick?), and they experiment with size, shape, and color. Small muscle coordination is developed by cutting out the valentine picture or heart and gluing it on the stick.

Materials & tools

red construction paper	felt-tip markers, crayons, or paints &
scissors	brushes
old valentine cards cut apart	paper cup or small cardboard box
glue	tape
ribbon or yarn or paper doilies	popsicle sticks
scraps of cloth or lace	

1. Cut out some hearts or pictures of valentines. Make six or more.
2. Glue hearts or pictures on popsicle sticks. Glue one on each side so both sides will look pretty.
3. Put your popsicle flowers in a paper cup or box. Cover the cup or box with red paper, and glue some hearts on it. If you use a small paper cup, you will need to put something heavy like a small rock or a piece of clay in the bottom to keep it from tipping over.

I learned . . .

I learned how to cut and glue carefully.
I learned how to make different kinds of valentines.

Egg characters for Easter

Making paper Easter eggs is another way children experience the fun of decorating an egg. The large egg is easier for the children to decorate. If time is short, the eggs can be made and painted ahead of time.

This activity can be an inexpensive substitute for the more elaborate process of dyeing real eggs.

Poster paint is the best paint to use. The paint needs to be thick enough so that it won't soak into the paper egg. Give the egg one coat and let it dry thoroughly before trying to paint or paste designs on it. A hair dryer can speed the drying process.

Through making and decorating their Easter eggs, children learn to visualize the size and shape of an egg, and they add descriptive words—such as *top*, *bottom*, *middle*, *center*, *oval*, and *egg-shaped*—to their vocabulary. They also develop a sense of time as they experience how long it takes the egg to dry. If appropriate, you can tell the children something about the holiday of Easter.

Materials & tools

1 large sheet of newsprint or 3 paper towels	paint in pastel colors
masking tape	construction paper cut in 2″-×-12″ strips
6″ string	glue

assortment of ribbon, lace, beads,
   yarn, small pieces of colored
   paper or stickers
	scissors

	felt-tip markers
	paint brushes

1. Wad up sheets of newsprint or paper towels, and roll them into the shape of a very large egg.
2. Put a piece of masking tape around the middle. Put another piece of tape around the egg, starting at the top and going down to the bottom and back to the top. Add more tape. Shape the egg as you apply the tape.
3. Put a spot of glue at the top of the egg. Make a loop with the string and tie the ends together into a knot.
4. Place the knot in the spot of glue. Put some tape around it to hold the string in place.
5. Paint your egg. Let it dry.

6. Print your name on the strip of construction paper, and decorate it any way you want. Tape or glue it to make a tube. This tube will hold your egg upright so you can decorate it.

7. Set your egg in the paper tube as a stand. Now you can add any decorations you want to your egg.

Variations

- Make an Easter egg tree. Hang the eggs on the tree.
- Make an egg mobile using a wire-hanger, paper plate, or crossed dowel sticks.

I learned . . .

I learned how to shape paper to look like an egg.
I learned how to make my egg stand up.
I learned how to decorate an egg.

27 Ages 5 and up

Mother's Day flowers

This craft—and, the *Father's Day Pocket Card*—will help to increase children's awareness of ways to help around the house. They will learn words associated with work, and the project will make them think about what they can do to help their mothers. Most of all, the children will enjoy giving their mothers a useful gift.

NOTE: You will have to be sensitive to children who have no mother in the home or who have several women who play the role of mother. Allow such children to select an alternative craft or to present the card to an important woman in their life—or even to their father.

You need to have a model for the children to see before they start this craft. If your group is large or time is limited, write down several tasks on the popsicle sticks and let the children select which ones to put on the flowers.

When the children select tasks, read them aloud, then have the children "read" them back to you. Do this several times to be sure the child understands the tasks and can "read" them from memory. This is an important step in learning to read.

Materials & tools

3 pieces of construction paper, 8″×9″, in pastel colors for flowers
3 popsicle sticks

paper cup or small clay pot
scissors
felt-tip markers or crayons

1. On the construction paper, draw three pretty flowers—daisies, tulips, sunflowers, etc.—and cut them out.
2. Glue each flower on a separate popsicle stick.
3. Think of three nice things you can do for your mother and write one thing on each stick. Here are some things you could do:

> I will pick up my toys.
> I will hang up my clothes.
> I will help wash the dishes.
> I will help wash the car.
> I will set the table.
> I will clean up my room.

4. Put the popsicle flowers in a paper cup or flower pot. If you use a paper cup, put something heavy in the bottom so it won't tip over. Give this pretty pot of flowers to your mother on Mother's day.

I learned . . .

I learned some ways I can help my mother.
I learned how to make a nice gift for my mother.
I learned how to glue paper flowers on popsicle sticks.

28 Ages 5 and up

Father's Day pocket card

This craft—and, the *Mother's Day Flowers*—will help to increase children's awareness of ways to help around the house. They will learn words associated with work, and the project will make them think about what they can do to help their fathers. Most of all, the children will enjoy giving their fathers a useful gift.

NOTE: You will have to be sensitive to children who have no father in the home or who have several men who play the role of father. Allow such children to select an alternative craft or to present the card to an important man in their life—or even to their mother.

You need to have a model for the children to see before they start this craft. If your group is large or time is limited, write down several tasks on the popsicle sticks and let the children select which ones to put on the garden tools.

Have the children tell you what they want the inside of the card to say. When the children select tasks, read them aloud, then have the children "read" them back to you. Do this several times to be sure the child understands the tasks and can "read" them from memory. This is an important step in learning to read.

Materials & tools

1 piece of light blue construction
   paper, 9"×12", for card
1 piece of dark blue construction
   paper, 4"×5", for pocket
3 pieces of construction paper, any
   color, approximately 3"×4"

3 popsicle sticks
scissors
felt-tip markers or crayons
glue

1. On the dark blue construction paper, make a picture of the back pocket on a pair of blue jeans. Make it big enough to hold three popsicle sticks.
2. Fold the light blue construction paper in half like a card.
3. Glue the pocket on the front of the card. Put the glue around the edges of three sides. The top needs to be open just like a real pocket.
4. Draw a picture of a rake, a shovel, and a broom.
5. Glue each picture on the end of separate popsicle sticks.
6. Think of some nice ways to help your father, and write one on each stick.
7. Put the garden tools in the pocket. Write something nice inside, and give it to your dad on Father's day.

I learned . . .

I learned some ways I can help my father.
I learned how to make a Father's Day card.

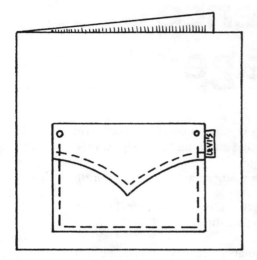

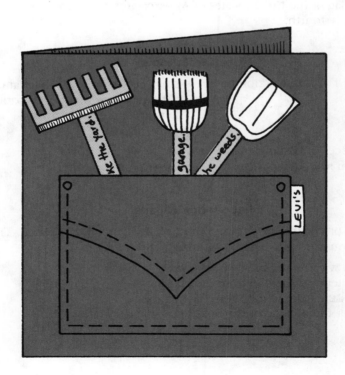

29 Ages 3 and up

Independence Day collage

One of the most creative things a child can do is make a collage. When you supply the proper materials, the child is free to make anything he or she wants. Even 3-year-olds love to create this kind of a collage.

Avoid comparing one child's work with another. Since each is a form of individual expression, there are never any bad collages.

Discuss the word *collage*, and tell the children that it is a form of modern art. Have the children repeat the word several times so that they can tell their parents what they have made.

Talk about the colors red, white, and blue, and about patriotism. Have a flag where the children can see it. If you have children from other countries, explain that this is the flag of the United States of America and we celebrate our independence day on July fourth.

Materials & tools

thin cardboard or construction paper, 6″ × 9″
scissors
glue

small pieces of red, white, and blue tissue paper or colored paper
felt-tip markers or crayons

1. Twist the pieces of tissue paper to look like flowers or bows.
2. Arrange them in a design or picture. Glue them on the paper.

Shadow-box collage

See the illustration for this variation to the Independence Day Collage. The only extra material you need is a shoe box for each child.

1. Line the box with red, white or blue paper.
2. Arrange the items in the box to make a design.
3. Glue them to the sides and bottom of the box.
4. Paint or cover the outside of the box. Put some decorations on it.

I learned . . .

I learned that the colors in our flag are red, white, and blue.
I learned the word *collage*.

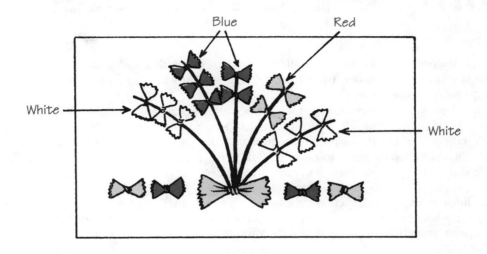

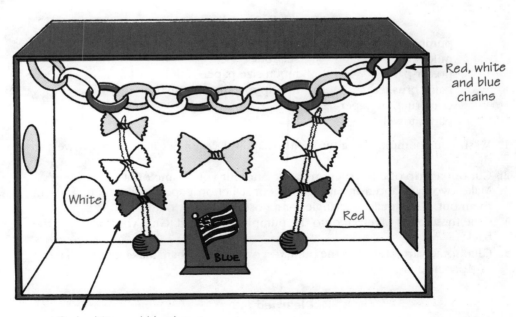

30 Ages 4 and up

Pumpkins on parade

This craft is good to make around Halloween when pumpkins and gourds are available. It requires less supervision than carving with a knife and allows the child to do more of the project.

If felt-tip markers are used be sure they are nontoxic in case the pumpkin is to be cooked later. If the pumpkin is not intended to be eaten, paint can be used (although felt-tip markers are easier with a group). Make the paint thick. If necessary, add a little kitchen cleanser to make it stick to the pumpkin.

If the skin of the pumpkin is not cut and the pumpkin stays dry, the pumpkin or gourd will last for weeks without molding.

In addition to expanding their vocabulary with words such as *pumpkin, Halloween, jack-o-lantern*, etc., this project will allow children to be creative and to develop a positive self-image, especially if the project is displayed or used as a Halloween decoration.

Materials & tools

pumpkin or gourd	yarn for hair, yellow and brown
mild soap	scissors
poster paint	lunch-size paper sack for hat
paint brushes	felt-tip markers or crayons
construction paper	glue
paper towels	

1. Wash your pumpkin or gourd with soap and water. Set it on paper towels to dry.
2. Cut out a strip of construction paper, and put your name on it.
3. Make two eyes and a mouth out of construction paper. Color them and cut them out. Then make a triangle for a nose, and cut it out.
4. Glue these parts of a face onto the pumpkin or gourd. Glue your name on the back.
5. Glue some yarn on top of the pumpkin or gourd for hair. Make a funny hat out of a paper sack.

I learned . . .

I learned how to decorate a pumpkin.
I learned the words *pumpkin, Halloween,* and *jack-o-lantern.*

31 Ages 5 and up

Thanksgiving turkeys

To make the turkey cups, you need to have a model for the children to see. This is a hard craft to visualize before it is made.

If the group is large or time is limited, you might want to copy the pattern or have available cardboard patterns that can be traced. Make a pattern for the head and wattle of the turkey. (You might want to explain to children that the *wattle* is the fold of skin that hangs down the turkey's neck just below the beak.)

The children can do the cutting and the gluing of the parts. They might need help gluing the feathers to the rectangle and taping the rectangle around the cup.

As you make this turkey, talk about how turkeys came to be a symbol of Thanksgiving. Talk about sharing things we have made.

Making these Thanksgiving turkeys, the children develop the skills of tracing and cutting, learn about Thanksgiving and turkeys, and develop a positive self-image through adding their projects to their family's Thanksgiving celebration.

Materials & tools

3 oz. paper cup
1 piece each of green, orange, & yellow construction paper, 3″× 5″
red construction paper for wattle, approximately 2″×2″
brown construction paper for head, approximately 3″×4″

brown construction paper rectangle, 2¹/₂″×8″
transparent tape
pencil
glue
scissors
paper clips
felt-tip markers or crayons

1. Carefully bend each piece of green, yellow, and orange paper lengthwise. Don't flatten it out; just bend it. The result will be 3″×2¹/₂″.
2. Cut the long folded side every ¹/₂″. These loops will become the feathers. Do the same with the other strips of colored paper.
3. Glue or tape the cut paper feathers to one end of the brown rectangle. Tape each color on top of the other.
4. Wrap the brown rectangle around the paper cup. Be sure the feathers stand up. Tape the rectangle so it doesn't slip.
5. Now you're ready to make the turkey head. Fold the brown paper in half. Lay the turkey head pattern down on the paper. Line up the flat top of the turkey head on top of the fold in the paper. When you cut out the turkey head, you will actually be cutting two pieces that will be joined together at the top of the head.

6. Be sure the turkey head pattern is in the right place on your folded paper, then trace around it.
7. Cut the head out carefully.
8. Unfold the paper. Draw an eye on each side of the turkey's head.
9. Spread the neck so that each side fits on the paper cup on the side opposite the feathers.
10. Trace the pattern for the wattle on red paper and cut it out. Fold the wattle in half. Glue it just under the turkey's beak.

You now have a turkey with a cup in the middle. The cup can be filled with nuts, candy, mints or small fall flowers to decorate the table for Thanksgiving.

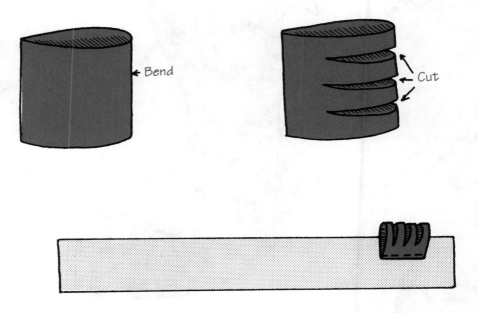

Fold

Fold

Variations

- Use a pine cone for the body of the turkey. Stick the folded feathers in between the petals of the pine cone. Cut the neck so that it can be inserted in the petals also.
- Use an apple or an orange for the turkey body. Tape the feathers to the back, tape the head to the front.

I learned . . .

I learned that turkeys have feathers and a wattle.
I learned what turkeys mean to Thanksgiving.
I learned how to make a decoration for the Thanksgiving table.

32 Ages 4 and up

Pine cone people

This is a great craft for Christmas gifts, party favors, or to tie onto Christmas packages. If time permits, take the children on a nature walk to gather the pine cones, pine needles, acorns, and twigs.

Have a few models ready to show the children before you begin this craft. Talk about how you made these, and how they can make their own. Theirs do not need to look just like yours.

Place the materials needed in front of the children. Encourage them to experiment before they begin gluing the pieces in place on the pine cone.

If you want more color, the pine cones can be painted with poster paint and let to dry before making elves and people. (You might want to do this in a separate session.)

Materials & tools

pine cones	yarn
pine needles	thin cardboard
acorns	scissors
buttons, beads, or movable eyes	glue
colored construction paper	felt-tip markers
pipe cleaners	

1. Cut a circle of cardboard as large as the fattest part of the pine cone.
2. Set the pine cone in the middle of the circle. If the pine cone won't stand up on its own, get two beans for feet. Experiment where the beans need to be to help the pine cone stand up. Glue the pine cone onto the circle. Glue two beans or buttons onto the circle to make the feet.
3. Make a head of an acorn, a bead, or the top of the pine cone.
4. Glue on beans for eyes (or use movable eyes).
5. Put a spot of glue on top and stick some yarn in it to make hair, or glue on pine needles to make straight hair.

Variations

- Make other pine cone critters the same way. You can make hats for some. You can make a book for one of them to hold on pipe-cleaner arms.
- You can make some of the pine cones look like porcupines by using pine needles or toothpicks.
- Paint some of the elves red, green, or white and use them for Christmas tree ornaments or tie them onto a package.

I learned . . .

I learned how to make pine cone people.
I learned to make each one look different.
I learned to make pine cone animals, too.

String painting Christmas wrap

String painting can be done by all ages. It's a very creative way to experiment with colors. Using just three colors, children can make interesting pictures, and no two pictures turn out exactly the same.

The painting needs to be done on a table covered with plastic or on a pad of newspapers. The children need to use painting aprons to protect their clothing. Old shirts worn backwards can be used instead of aprons. Although this craft is somewhat messy, it is creative fun and a great way to make Christmas wrapping paper.

In addition to learning how to make string painting, children will learn how to create a design instead of a picture, and how colors change when mixed together.

Materials & tools

yarn or string, about 12" per color
3 colors of poster paint
newsprint or butcher paper

3 bowls
(one for each color of paint)

1. Pour each color of poster paint into a small bowl, such as a margarine plastic tub.
2. Hold both ends of the yarn, and dip the center of the yarn into the paint.
3. Drag the yarn across the paper, letting the paint make a design on the paper.
4. Repeat this step with the second color and a fresh piece of yarn, then with the third color and a fresh piece of yarn. Notice how the color changes when it crosses another color.
5. Put each of the paint strings on one sheet of paper in a circle or some other design when you have finished the picture above. You might need to dip them into the paint again to be sure they still have wet paint on them.
6. Place the second sheet of paper on top of the first one and press it down with your hand. Rub all over the top paper, but don't move it.
7. Carefully peel up the top paper, and remove the strings. Now you have two more string paintings.

I learned . . .

I learned how to make my own gift wrap.
I learned how to paint with yarn instead of with a paint brush.
I learned how colors change when they are mixed.

Fold and press

Ages 3 and up

Christmas ornaments

To do this craft with a group of children, two or more adults are needed. One leader helps the children with their dried arrangements while another adult takes one child at a time to the paint center to dip their arrangements. Be sure the area you will be working in is well-ventilated.

If possible, hang the painted objects outside to dry. If not, you will need to have plenty of newspapers spread on the floor so that paint drips will not damage the floor or furniture. Make a path of newspapers from the dipping area to the drying area. Both children and adults need aprons or old shirts to protect their clothing.

You will need old rags and paint thinner to clean up hands and spills. Remember that paint thinner is dangerous. Do not have it where the children can reach it. When you are finished with them, place any rags with paint thinner in a tightly sealed container.

Through doing this closely supervised craft, children learn to experiment with berries, seed pods, and leaves to make an arrangement and expand their vocabulary with the word *corsage* and the names of seeds and berries.

Materials & tools

an assortment of seed pods, leaves, dried berries, small pine cones, small pine branches
empty gallon bucket or can
clean rags
Christmas ribbon for bow

silver or gold oil-based paint
string about 18″ long
water
paint thinner
newspapers or old shower curtain

1. Fill the container with water about 2″ from the top. Set in on a pad of newspapers or an old shower curtain. Spread newspapers on the floor to protect it from paint drips and spills.
2. Pour about 2 tablespoons of silver or gold paint on the water. Do NOT stir. Let the paint float on top of the water.
3. Select pods, berries, and leaves to make a pretty arrangement. Place them with the stems all facing the same way.

4. Tie the string tightly around the stems so the arrangement will not fall apart when it is dipped in the paint and water. Leave about 8″ of string so you can hold the arrangement as you dip it into the paint and water.
5. Lower the arrangement by the string into the paint. Move it around until it is well coated with the gold or silver paint. Tie the arrangement on a line with newspapers underneath to catch any drips.
6. Let the arrangement dry for at least a day. Remove it from the line and tie a pretty Christmas bow around the stems. You now have a pretty Christmas decoration or corsage to give as a gift.

I learned . . .

I learned the word *corsage*.
I learned to use berries and pods to make a corsage.
I learned that oil paint will float on the top of water.

Index